PRAISE FOR M. L. BUCHMAN

One of our favorite authors.

— RT BOOK REVIEWS

Buchman has catapulted his way to the top tier of my favorite authors.

— FRESH FICTION

A favorite author of mine. I'll read anything that carries his name, no questions asked. Meet your new favorite author!

— THE SASSY BOOKSTER, FLASH OF FIRE

M.L. Buchman is guaranteed to get me lost in a good story.

— THE READING CAFE, WAY OF THE WARRIOR: NSDQ

I love Buchman's writing. His vivid descriptions bring everything to life in an unforgettable way.

— PURE JONEL, HOT POINT

BETWEEN SHADOW AND SOUL

WHITE HOUSE PROTECTION FORCE STORY

M. L. BUCHMAN

Buchman Bookworks

Other works by M. L. Buchman:

<u>White House Protection Force</u>
Off the Leash
On Your Mark
In the Weeds

<u>The Night Stalkers</u>
MAIN FLIGHT
The Night Is Mine
I Own the Dawn
Wait Until Dark
Take Over at Midnight
Light Up the Night
Bring On the Dusk
By Break of Day
WHITE HOUSE HOLIDAY
Daniel's Christmas
Frank's Independence Day
Peter's Christmas
Zachary's Christmas
Roy's Independence Day
Damien's Christmas
AND THE NAVY
Christmas at Steel Beach
Christmas at Peleliu Cove
5E
Target of the Heart
Target Lock on Love
Target of Mine
Target of One's Own

<u>Firehawks</u>
MAIN FLIGHT
Pure Heat
Full Blaze
Hot Point
Flash of Fire
Wild Fire
SMOKEJUMPERS
Wildfire at Dawn
Wildfire at Larch Creek
Wildfire on the Skagit

<u>Delta Force</u>
Target Engaged
Heart Strike
Wild Justice
Midnight Trust

<u>Where Dreams</u>
Where Dreams are Born
Where Dreams Reside
Where Dreams Are of Christmas
Where Dreams Unfold
Where Dreams Are Written

<u>Eagle Cove</u>
Return to Eagle Cove
Recipe for Eagle Cove
Longing for Eagle Cove
Keepsake for Eagle Cove

<u>Henderson's Ranch</u>
Nathan's Big Sky
Big Sky, Loyal Heart
Big Sky Dog Whisperer

<u>Love Abroad</u>
Heart of the Cotswolds: England
Path of Love: Cinque Terre, Italy

<u>Dead Chef Thrillers</u>
Swap Out!
One Chef!
Two Chef!

<u>Deities Anonymous</u>
Cookbook from Hell: Reheated
Saviors 101

<u>SF/F Titles</u>
The Nara Reaction
Monk's Maze
the Me and Elsie Chronicles

<u>Strategies for Success (NF)</u>
Managing Your Inner Artist/Writer
Estate Planning for Authors

Short Story Series by M. L. Buchman:

The Night Stalkers
The Night Stalkers
The Night Stalkers 5E
The Night Stalkers CSAR
The Night Stalkers Wedding Stories

Firehawks
The Firehawks Lookouts
The Firehawks Hotshots
The Firebirds

Delta Force
Delta Force Short Stories

US Coast Guard
US Coast Guard

White House Protection Force
White House Protection Force Short Stories

Where Dreams
Where Dreams Short Stories

Eagle Cove
Eagle Cove Short Story

Henderson's Ranch
Henderson's Ranch Short Stories

Dead Chef Thrillers
Dead Chef Short Stories

Deities Anonymous
Deities Anonymouse Short Stories

SF/F Titles
The Future Night Stalkers
Single Titles

I should have stayed in the Congo. Michael was careful not to make eye contact as he stood up from the briefing table and left the White House Situation Room. At least there they were just committing genocide —which could be stopped if enough pressure was applied. In here, they were committing politics.

He waited at the security desk while they tracked down his cell phone—none allowed inside the Situation Room. He glared at the mahogany-dark wall so that he didn't put his hands around someone's throat. Even his own at this point if it would get him out of here faster.

How he'd let Brigadier General Andhauer talk him into coming out of the field to take over command of Delta Force Michael would never know.

Actually, he knew exactly how.

"Nobody knows the shadow world of Delta the way you do, Michael. You want *the* hallowed name in this outfit? It isn't mine. It's Colonel Michael Gibson. Shit. If the truth ever got out about all the medals you've been awarded for black ops… Seriously, I can't trust anyone else to keep Delta out at the tip of the spear."

But Andhauer had always been the politician. Even back when they'd both been raw recruits fresh out of the six-month Operator Training Course, he'd been able to talk the instructors into looking the other way for all kinds of escapades. It was still a mystery quite how he'd kept the team out of trouble after blowing up a general's Land Rover as part of a graduation test take-down demonstration. Yes, the general shouldn't have had tinted windows and parked it in the front of the target building, but they'd all known it was his.

"Should have bought American," Andhauer had joked privately after convincing the general to be actually impressed at how rapidly and thoroughly they'd destroyed the target vehicle and the "enemy nest" inside the building. They hadn't just killed it; they'd blown the shit out of it so badly that the largest remaining piece was half of an engine block. The fireball had been a beauty. It also *had* been the ultimate distraction, covering their high-speed forced entry of the building.

All Michael had ever been was a Delta field operator.

And there wasn't a single person in this room, perhaps in the entire White House, who remembered what it meant to be on the front line. The Joint Chiefs' agendas weren't exactly uninformed, but they sure didn't factor the one-point-three million active-duty men and women into their planning. Or any other piece of reality that he could identify. The top-tier ones at the Pentagon weren't much better.

That did it. He was never again going to trust someone wearing more than two stars.

For two years he'd been the sole voice of "The Field" in these meetings. At first he'd felt he was reawakening their memories of when they too had served—at least for those who had. Political appointees and intelligence agents turned agency directors he could almost forgive even if he didn't understand them. They had never known the lessons that only war could teach.

But the effect had worn off soon enough. Now even the battle-bred generals barely looked at him except to ask if Delta could perform such-and-such.

"No. That's more appropriate for regular forces."

"No. That's for the Green Beret negotiators. They do the civilian cooperation missions."

"No, you goddamn idiots. Don't you understand the mission profiles of your own elite counter-terrorism force? We're the best shooters there are. We can go deeper undercover than your best CIA agents and come up shooting. You want hostages? Call out the Rangers. You want a mission where no one knows we were even there but the target gets obliterated? That's us. You wanted bin Laden —without all the news coverage and tell-all book crap? You should have called goddamn Delta not the SEALs." He probably shouldn't have said the last with General Jefferson in the room as he'd been a DEVGRU—SEAL Team 6— commander before taking command of SOCOM. Whatever else was going on, General Jefferson ran Special Operations Command which still made him Michael's boss.

He tried to remember the last time he'd lost his

temper…and couldn't. Not even all the way back in high school. Claudia had said this job was changing him, but he'd written that off to her hormones from pregnancy. He should have known better than to doubt Claudia's judgement about anything.

Michael took his phone from the National Security Council watch officer and inspected the message queue carefully. Asshole—delete. Jerk—forward to his assistant. Narcissistic political climber? Sick of him, Michael set up an auto-forward on that number to go to the Naval Observatory time-of-day recording.

Finally! Claudia. Just a thumbs up. The only thing that mattered these days.

When had he become a maniac about her health? She was the most capable woman and pilot he'd ever met. She could survive for weeks in the desert starting out with nothing more than a sharp stick. But the day she'd told him of her pregnancy, he'd begun researching the consequences more thoroughly than a take-down mission deep in denied territory.

Thumbs up. Good. He ignored the rest of the message queue, jammed the phone in his pocket, and strode out the double door into the West Wing lobby. He wanted to be nowhere near this place by the time the next person came out.

Four steps outside the door, a dog sat at attention looking straight at him. It was so unexpected that he actually stumbled to a halt. Staffers and official visitors swirled around the seated dog as no one would dare displace *this* animal. If he curled up and slept there, security would quietly put up a sign post so that no one tripped over him.

"Hey, Zackie." He'd always liked the First Dog—an immaculately groomed brown-and-white Sheltie. He showed that it was mutual with a happy tail wag as Michael bent down to pet him. "Where's your master?" There was some question if that was the First Family or their dog handler and part-time First Nanny Dilya Stevenson.

In answer Zackie popped to his feet and began trotting deeper into the West Wing rather than out of it.

"No way, Zackie." Never Zack, because that was the President's first name. The First Lady had revealed her sense of humor by naming their dog after her husband so that they both responded every time either was called. "I'm headed out of here."

The dog stopped and gave him a puzzled look when he didn't follow. A tilt of his head asking what was wrong with him. As if Michael had any idea.

He pointed at his own chest and then toward the beckoning exit.

Still watching Michael over his shoulder as he took another step toward the stairs, Zackie almost took out an intern loaded down with an armful of files.

"She's got him trained up a treat now," a woman's voice spoke close beside him. It's owner was a slender brunette. US Secret Service emblazoned across her chest and a scruffy mutt in a service vest at her side.

At Michael's glance, the woman grinned.

"Have to admit a lot of that's my and Thor's fault. Colby and Rex started working with Dilya before they went to NASA to take over security there, but we're the ones who kept working with her. Dilya's really hard to say no to when she starts asking all of those questions. I must say, that girl is a bottomless pit of questions."

Michael glanced down at the woman's Secret Service dog. The dust mop of mutt looked as proud as the USSS dog handler. As they'd saved the President's life in his first week or so on the job, Michael supposed the look was deserved.

Zackie remained poised in the middle of the hallway, one foot still in the air.

"Don't make him wait too long," the woman winked. "He's still only a Sheltie. If he gets excited he tends to forget things."

She headed off toward the Secret Service Ready Room.

Dilya. That girl could make a man's head hurt. Ten-year-old Uzbekistani orphans were not supposed to be as smart as that girl had been. Had been, because now at seventeen she was several times smarter. Growing up first on a Night Stalkers forward operating base where he'd been stationed and then in the White House as nanny to two administrations had also given her the resources to hone those observational skills that had kept her alive in a war zone.

Michael heard voices sounding loudly behind him. The others exiting from the latest meeting, complaining about him—probably plotting against him as if *he* was the enemy. All their noise was cut off abruptly by his unexpected presence still in the West Wing lobby, as if they thought that wouldn't *prove* that he was the topic they were discussing. He double-checked his critics by glancing at the shiny brass "Men's Room" plaque across the hall. It indeed reflected an array of green and blue uniforms that most of those men no longer deserved to wear.

Fine. He turned smartly and followed the dog. Most of them would be unable to follow. Michael still held a White House "All Areas" security badge—a holdover from the prior administration that the current administration had renewed. The other military personnel in the meeting hadn't had such clearance except for the Chairman of the Joint Chiefs. He was the only rational one left in the room but Michael didn't want to talk to him either, even though it was easy to respect him.

Without once turning to acknowledge the men who had streamed out of the Situation Room behind him, Michael strode over to the waiting Zackie.

"Dilya?" he asked the dog. At least he hoped that's where the dog was headed. Hell, if it got him out of here, he'd follow the dog straight to the President.

He'd take the tongue loll and Zackie setting off again as a good sign.

CHAPTER 2

The dog led him up one flight, out the doors to the West Colonnade, and into the Residence via the Palm Room.

As he stepped past one of the palm trees, Dilyana Stevenson slipped up beside him, then tossed Zackie a treat. He'd seen her of course: the room's only occupant other than a Secret Service agent. She'd been out of his sightlines, but not the agent's—who had been watching her hiding place. Michael considered pointing out what gave her away, but decided to let her have the win.

"How do you hide dressed like that?"

At seventeen, the girl had probably topped out just a few inches under his own five-ten. She'd kept her black, curly hair long and was dressed like what he supposed was standard attire for an American teen at the White House. Forest green leggings that matched her sneakers and one of the three color swathes of her blouse. The skirt's dark blue somehow making the outfit cohesive.

Nothing could hide those searching green eyes offset against her dark complexion.

"People see what they expect."

A glance at Dilya would reveal a lovely teen going about her life. She even wore white headphone wires that traced down into one of her pockets that he wagered were never actually turned on when something of interest could be happening. The girl probably had dark-wired headphones to stand out when she wore light-colored outfits. Modern camouflage. That startled him enough to look at her askance.

"What?"

"Just realized that if Claudia has a girl—"

"—and she was anything like me, then you're in for a load of trouble, *Dad*."

Michael's throat went drier than the Libyan desert. *Dad?* He was always fully prepped for a mission before he deployed. This time? How was he supposed to prepare for a mission of *Dad?* He was in serious trouble.

Dilya grinned happily. Mindreading was one of her many uncanny skills. "Don't worry. Claudia's freaking too."

He resisted asking how she knew that. Then he remembered a note on Claudia's calendar of sea glass photos from last week, "10 am archery." Claudia had trained Dilya to shoot a bow and arrow when they were still all overseas and he knew they still got together on occasion for that. "Who shot best?"

Dilya sounded a loud raspberry as they walked beneath the broad marble arches of the Ground Floor's

Central Hall. "Emily was in town. Neither of us stood a chance."

Michael wished he'd seen that. Emily Beale, Dilya, and his own Claudia proving just how lethal women could be. But he'd been in yet another meeting of the endless meetings that had become his life. Andhauer hadn't been kidding about needing someone to hold the line for Delta —he'd never fought a harder battle.

"I'm sorry I missed her." It was partly Emily's doing that he'd finally accepted the promotion to command Delta. Perhaps she could help him figure out how to fix what was going on now. He should've of thought of that.

"She is pretty awesome, isn't she?"

She was. Emily had been the first woman to break into the Special Operations Night Stalkers helicopter 160th regiment. She'd since had two kids and retired to her in-law's horse ranch in Montana. Mostly retired. He made a mental note to talk to her soon.

Michael almost tripped over Zackie himself when Dilya and the dog took an unexpected turn into the North Hall, swung around the back of the Curator's Office, and down a flight of stairs. He'd never been in the White House Residence's basement before.

He considered asking where she was leading him, and why. But with each step away from the Situation Room, he became more himself. Knowing those questions would be answered when they'd arrived wherever Dilya was leading, there was no need to ask. There were plenty of objects about if a weapon was needed on short notice—an unlikely scenario inside the White House: a line of folding chairs, a heavy-bottomed stanchion with a retractable belt in the top, and the slight catch in the swing of Dilya's skirt that said she had a knife strapped to her thigh under there.

"Are you still carrying the Cold Steel Recon?"

Dilya nodded. "I've been taking lessons with one of the Secret Service agents. I'm getting pretty good with it."

Michael made another mental note to teach his own child knifework as soon as they were old enough. "Huh."

"What?"

He hadn't realized he'd come to a halt. "I think it finally just sunk in that I'm going to have a kid of my own soon. I know nothing about kids."

"You know me."

"Your mom rescued you when you were ten, and you were never a kid, kid." And now she was a very striking young woman and heaven help anyone who underestimated her as being "merely" a teen.

Dilya smiled at him. "Not a lot of people know that about me. You, the old Night Stalkers team, and a few others. Everyone else thinks I'm just the First Nanny."

"Not Zackie." Michael surprised himself with a tease.

"No. He thinks I'm the Goddess of the Dog Treats." Dilya continued leading them downward into the subbasement.

He considered the spaces that he'd cataloged during their descent.

The kitchens and the chocolate and carpentry shops had been on the ground floor. He'd seen those before.

The subbasement mezzanine had included mostly storage areas and electrical service. There'd been two distinct sounds on this level, the massive air conditioning system had sent low frequency vibrations through the well-insulated wall. The distant echoes of the dishwashers had come from the far end of the corridor, distorted enough to have turned at least two corners. The rest of the floor remained relatively quiet.

The lowest subbasement repeated the air conditioning —a two-story installation—and at the far end of the main corridor he spotted evidence of the White House laundry services. An usher, immaculate in her dark blue skirt and blazer stepped out of some waiting room and hurried up stairs at the far end of the corridor. This end was strictly mechanical services. A sudden hum identified elevator machinery as it engaged to move someone between the Residence's upper stories. It was a whole other world from the Residence that most people saw with its elegance and grand staterooms.

Dilya stopped at Mechanical Room 043 and, after carefully checking that they were alone, knocked. He raised an eyebrow at her and she looked a little sheepish when nothing happened.

"Sometimes we have to wait."

If Delta had taught him anything, it was how to wait. Patience was one of the most essential skills that Delta taught.

Zackie, however, had other ideas and scratched at the door a few times impatiently.

After a long minute, the door opened.

CHAPTER 3

"Mechanical Room 043," was all he could think to say to the woman seated at a desk with knitting spread across her lap. She was almost invisible in the apparently well-lit room. A small lamp shone upon her bright green yarn. Subtle track lighting lit the bookcases that covered every wall. Yet no light at all fell upon the woman seated behind the desk. If it had ever been a Mechanical Room, it was far in 043's past.

The woman was seated in the only shadow in the room, clearly marking her as the most important object in the space. Little showed other than a hint of brilliant blue eyes.

"Ah, Colonel Gibson. A unique pleasure indeed. Welcome." Her voice, deeply husky, was also slightly thinned with age. The lightness of her long hair in the shadows might be gray rather than blonde. "Please, take a seat." The hands holding the knitting were lightly spotted with age, confirming the hypothesis.

He waited without moving, though Dilya sat easily in

one of the two small chairs facing the desk. The space wasn't large enough to accommodate a third. She did it with an ease of long familiarity. Zackie also went over to greet the woman and received a head pat for his troubles.

"Dilya trusts you very deeply, Colonel. Even her parents have not been brought to meet me."

Dilya was looking down at her folded hands, her hair shaken forward to hide her face. He knew that she only did that when embarrassed or wanted to assess a situation without appearing to. She was familiar with the space and the woman, so embarrassment seemed unlikely.

He considered Dilya's penchant for finding the primary source of information. A quick glance revealed that she'd done so once again. The bulk of the texts in the wall-to-wall bookcases covering all four walls were about spies and spycraft. Tucked into odd corners were microcameras, a tiny 2.7mm Kolibri pistol (which shot the smallest caliber bullet ever manufactured—just a third the size of a .22), and other minute paraphernalia.

Then he noticed the slotted flash suppressor indicating that a rifle lay atop one of the cases. After a glance for permission—which was answered by what might have been a shadowed smile—he extracted the weapon. Four feet of Soviet Dragunov SVD sniper rifle.

"Wooden stock. Skeletonized. Chambered for 7.62x54mmR with a ten-round magazine and a PSO-1 scope. Unusually light and well-balanced for what it was. A masterful weapon to find in the White House subbasement... I don't recognize the serial numbering sequence. The standard ones use a letter prefix and a three- or five-digit number. This only has two digits."

"It is the seventeenth of the two hundred originally built for evaluation in 1963," her husky voice had taken on a curiously soft quality.

"A truly unique weapon." He didn't ask how she'd come by it and she didn't offer. He considered as he replaced it on the shelf—with everything *except* the flash suppressor out of sight.

One of the original two hundred.

Either she had once been a Russian sharpshooter… But that didn't fit the contents of the library. Spycraft. She'd been a spy stationed within the old Soviet Union. The original Dragunovs, those that weren't completely destroyed by the testing, would have been a serious collector's item. He still had in his own collection the tenth TAC 50 sniper rifle ever built. He also owned the second HK-416, that he'd helped develop with Heckler & Koch which was now standard issue for Delta Force. They'd offered him the first one, but he'd insisted that go to HK's lead designer.

Had she stolen the Dragunov? Or…had it been a gift? Ah.

"What was his name?"

The woman startled. Dilya's sudden shift of attention from behind her hair told him that was most unusual.

He brushed aside Dilya's hair as he sat and tucked it back over her shoulders. "It's not as concealing a trick as you think."

She grimaced, "It works on most people."

"The colonel is right, dear child. You have outgrown that ploy."

"So how do I see what I need to see without, you know…"

"Being seen?" Michael had given no thought to Emily's comments about how precocious Dilya had become. She had advanced far more than he'd realized—no wonder so many people underestimated her. "I expect that our nameless hostess could offer you some wisdom on that point."

He'd also noticed that during her revealing reaction of surprise, their hostess had started to raise her hand toward…

"That's a nice locket that you're wearing, ma'am."

The woman sighed and completed the aborted gesture to clasp it tightly. Tightly, but also tenderly. A gift, like the rifle, from someone she still cared about.

"You may call me Miss Watson." Then she turned to Dilya, "If you want a lesson in how to observe others without really looking, you may be better served by speaking with this young colonel."

Dilya glanced at him—sideways, evoking a laugh from their hostess.

"You're both youngsters to me. Your friend the colonel is far closer to your age than mine."

Michael hadn't considered that himself. His career was nearing its end. He'd never have the political savvy of Colin Powell or even Stan McChrystal. He'd always modeled himself after Chargin' Charlie Beckwith who'd conceived and founded Delta about the time Michael was born. Did the fact that Charlie had never made it past the rank of colonel tell him something about himself? He'd joined the Army at eighteen and gunned for Delta from the first day in Boot Camp. If he wasn't Delta, he was nothing.

But that Miss Watson was clearly working, decades on, gave him some form of hope.

It was a curious feeling, that almost…tickled. When had he lost track of hope?

CHAPTER 4

"If we must discuss Sergei…" Miss Watson sighed and gestured a hand to Dilya.

But the way the chairs had been placed, and with Zackie now curled up on her feet, Dilya was trapped close by the closed entry door.

"Allow me," Michael rose to his feet. "Back of the third shelf, or the fourth."

"Third," Miss Watson chuckled. "There is your man who sees without looking, Dilya. I'm afraid that I must ask how you know about my living room. I'm sure Dilya didn't tell you. She is charmingly protective of me."

"Which is among the highest praise I can think of. Dilya's trust is not given lightly."

With her hair back, Dilya's blush showed clearly despite her olive skin. He'd never considered that before, but it had been true. He'd witnessed her long internal battle before she finally trusted her adoptive mother. Somewhere along the way, without his noticing, she had granted that trust to him as well.

Michael rose and felt in the back corner of the waist-high third shelf. A pair of squat dictionaries provided just enough space to slip his hand into the shadowed space—invisible without bending down and using a flashlight. After he pressed the catch and began swinging the two bookcases back and to the sides, he gestured toward Zackie.

"After you pet him, he sniffed along only this one baseboard before returning to Dilya. He also glanced up at where he knew the catch was. You probably shouldn't store…" he walked over to the ceramic Snoopy lying atop his red doghouse and lifted the cookie jar's lid, "…doggie biscuits here if you wish to keep it private."

Zackie had followed him into the room, so Michael gave him a biscuit. The dog carried over to the dog bed close beside the large marble fireplace mantel. He stepped over to tap a switch beside the mantel and a merry gas flame snapped to life among the artificial logs inside the hearth's glass enclosure.

In contrast to the cluttered outer office, the wide-open bookcases had revealed a charming inner sanctum. It wasn't something he would have noticed before getting married, but he'd slowly been learning about Claudia's quiet joy in something cozy: a fireplace, a couch, a cup of tea. A vase of spring tulips sat close by a wingback chair. Flowers. He should try giving Claudia flowers and see what her reaction might be. Dilya came over and fussed with them, perhaps moving her favorite colors to the front. Yes, definitely buy Claudia a spring bouquet.

Pictures of women adorned the walls. It took only a few moments to see the pattern—spies. He recognized several of the more recent examples: the lovely Anna Chapman deported back to Russia in 2010, Jennifer Matthews who had led the hunt for bin Laden until she made a mistake and was killed along with six others by a bomb in 2009, Ana Montes who had spied for Cuba from inside the Defense Intelligence Agency for seventeen years and was now doing twenty-five years in a federal penitentiary. Every one of the women in these photos must have been spies for one country or another, one century or another.

The large oriental rug was a sharp contrast to the rough concrete finish of the outer office. Not outer office, outer *library*.

"Your picture isn't here."

Her smile spoke volumes.

So. Miss Watson was far more than she appeared. An American spy, who had received an incredibly rare Russian Dragunov SVD sniper rifle as a gift, had become a spycraft librarian in the White House subbasement.

"This is the center."

"The center?" Miss Watson asked with perfect nonchalance as she moved to make tea at a small nook in the corner of the room. Dilya was arranging a plate of chocolate chip cookies with the ease of long practice.

Michael sat in one of the guest chairs and observed the two women. Five or more decades apart in age, one slender with the posture of youth and the strength of a hard childhood and much practice since. The other slowly shifted as she relaxed. Her first, studied impression was a grandmotherly crone, bent over her knitting. But she moved with a former dancer's posture and lightness of stride. Her gray hair was a shining fall past her shoulders. She had clearly been tall and very attractive in her day.

"I have been in Emily's tactical command room at Henderson's Ranch," Michael offered a point of his own validation.

"Then you know what we are." Miss Watson delivered the tea as Dilya set the cookies on an ornately inlaid Indian table showing a herd of gray elephants grazing through a sparse forest and swimming in a blue-tinted river.

He considered the inclusion of Dilya in that statement: *what we are*. It had structural ramifications that he hadn't considered.

Michael had known of Emily's connection since the very beginning. And then he'd helped install Lauren, a former dog handler for Delta Force, as Emily's assistant. He knew that side of the operation.

"Just what is the scope of the White House Protection Force?"

CHAPTER 5

*M*iss Watson's smile as she settled in her chair told him that she was quite proud of what she'd built.

"It is as big as it needs to be—and no more," Michael guessed her answer before she gave it. "And?" he asked over her hearty laugh that seemed to strip away the years.

"Oh, it is *such* a joy to finally meet you, colonel. I have followed your career closely since the day you first landed in Afghanistan with Jawbreaker."

He'd still been a sergeant then, the only Delta operator to go in with that initial CIA team just two weeks after 9/11. No one should know about that. At least no one outside the CIA's black ops S.A.D.—Special Activities Division.

"Dilya?" Miss Watson made the question almost casual. Almost.

Dilya didn't miss it for a moment. "There are two dog handlers, the chocolate chef, and the driver of the

Presidential limo. An astronaut, and the new head of NASA's security."

Miss Watson nodded sagely as if that was good list, but Dilya continued.

"Secretary of State Matthews went to a lot of work setting it up while he was still President. That almost guarantees that Daniel and Alice know about it, though I'm pretty sure that President Zachary doesn't. Oh, and anything Secretary Matthews knows, his wife and the head of both of their protection details know. The two leads in the Secret Service office know to trust the WHPF's intelligence tips, even if they don't know who or what it is. They're actually awfully frustrated by that—it's kinda fun to watch. The head chef suspects. Oh, and I'm betting on the three White House librarians, of course."

Miss Watson blinked in surprise. "Anyone else I need to know about?"

Dilya shook her head.

"Shall I offer some others?" Michael asked. The technique of teasing typically eluded him, but this was an opportunity that was hard to resist.

They both blinked at him in surprise.

"Anything that Emily knows, her husband Mark knows."

"Nuh-uh," Dilya regressed to a teenage noise. "She'd never tell him."

"That's Mark's gift. He makes everyone think he's just a good old boy. I was there for the very first flight when he founded the 5D company. Mark misses nothing—ever. He knows exactly what his wife is doing even if he doesn't let on."

Dilya looked deflated but Michael couldn't resist.

"You're still missing three." But that was too much of a clue and she brightened again.

"Four if you count Zackie," who was now snoring on his dog bed.

CHAPTER 6

"I already was. It's only three. I may know about it, but I'm not *in* your WHPF."

And, as if a mission clock had just ticked to zero dark thirty, he felt himself go very still. This instinct had saved his life innumerable times on missions. It was odd that it had been triggered here, especially because he wasn't sure why.

There been no more than a hint. A shift.

It could be nothing, a bat winging by aloft on its hunt for mosquitos. Or it could be an enemy patrol crossing mere steps away from a hidden position.

Silence, perfect and complete silence revealed the truth more often than not.

There was, below conscious awareness, the basso thrum of the air conditioning systems. The cycling of the dishwashing equipment on the floor above sent a splash down through the thick lead pipes in the ceiling of Miss Watson's office. A brief rattle of dog tags marked Zackie's rolling over in his dog bed.

They had been discussing the White House Protection Force. His knowledge of it without any participation on his part.

He opened his eyes, having closed them to listen.

Miss Watson was no longer the charming matron with an unusual background. Now she watched him with all of the sharp-eyed assessment of a seasoned CIA field agent.

"An interesting thought, isn't it, colonel?"

"What thought?" What had he missed that she'd seen?

In his peripheral vision he could see Dilya glance back and forth between them. Then she giggled, completely breaking the tableau.

"What?"

She shook her head violently enough to flop hair over her face, but this time she shoved it aside. She only had to be told something once and she had it fully integrated. He tried to read her face, but she just shook her head.

"Ask Miss Watson about her Russian general. I love that story."

He waited, but Dilya understood the power of silence too well for that to work on her.

Finally, in unison, they turned to Miss Watson.

CHAPTER 7

"Lieutenant General Sergei Kulakov of Soviet Union's KGB First Directorate was one of Colonel General Aleksandr Sakharovsky's right hand men. He came to my attention as the head of the foreign intelligence service responsible for the US and Canada. Sergei was married to one of Sakharovsky's favorite cousins. She was a brainless little thug who spent her life drinking and betraying any gossip she could gain to the KGB."

Miss Watson looked so sad that Michael was sorry he'd even noticed the rifle in her collection. Dilya's wide eyes said she hadn't heard this part of it.

"I recruited him using his sadness. Even for a Russian he wore it more heavily than most. I was his 'Bright Flower'."

She slipped off the locket and handed it across. In one miniature photo, the brilliant blue eyes still matched the woman who wore it. Though the brightly blonde hair had turned gray, the same natural beauty remained. In the other photo, she sat in the lap of a Russian two-star general. Michael supposed he was handsome, though he'd never been able to tell with guys.

"He had an illegal translation of Pablo Neruda's love poetry and we would read it to each other. You should learn Russian, Dilya, it is a very sexy language."

"Um…I was already working on that." This time the blush told him nothing. Unless it was who she was learning it with. A boy?

"*Xavfsiz?*" He dredged up one of the few Uzbek words he remembered from her arrival in their Pakistan camp.

"Duh!"

As long as she was being safe, he'd let her worry about everything else. If Miss Watson understood the exchange, she gave no sign.

"For three years I lived very happily. I fed him leaked or declassified information before it was released and he fed me information on disinformation campaigns including forged documents supposedly from the CIA, but created by the Soviet Union to upset various governments. I still feel awful that I never once provided him with actionable intelligence, but his uncanny accuracy 'predicting' breaking news elevated him rapidly within the KGB nonetheless."

She toyed with the locket for a moment before sighing heavily.

"Do you have regrets, colonel?"

"Some, ma'am. Not many. Mostly lives I couldn't save."

"You are a fortunate man. I doubt there are many who

can say as much. Certainly not myself." She brushed her finger once more over the tiny picture before snapping it shut.

Michael rose and came forward to clasp the locket once more around her neck.

"Thank you, young man. I don't know how he was discovered. One day he was going to Moscow for meetings. That evening I received a call. The caller spoke the single word 'Run!' and then hung up. I didn't recognize the voice. I paused just long enough to confirm his arrest. I took his Dragunov. We had fired it at his Black Sea dacha many times for sport—he was a masterful shot. We both were. The competition was…" she glanced at Dilya then away, "invigorating."

"Meaning you had awesome shoot-out sex. I'm not *that* young, Miss Watson."

"Oh, but you are, my dear girl. Be that as it may, I raced his tiny fishing boat two hundred miles across the Black Sea through an awful winter storm to a miserable port town in eastern Turkey. They firebombed that beautiful dacha where we had spent three lovely years of our lives together. I can only imagine what he thought of my betrayal before they executed him for treason."

Michael recognized the strength in her as she sat perfectly upright and recovered her composure one small piece at a time.

Regrets.

What would he regret if he lived to be Miss Watson's age? Not defending Delta Force with his every breath? Being a lousy father?

Perhaps the key was in Dilya's laugh. What had she seen of his future in one of her flashes of insight. Why couldn't he get a glimpse despite all his straining?

He didn't know what his future was yet, but perhaps he could find out.

CHAPTER 8

"I was expecting a woman." Actually, Vladimir had never expected anyone of either gender to show up, ever.

"I'm a messenger for a woman seeking an answer to the past."

Vladimir nodded. It had been over fifty years, but there was no question what the quiet American was referring to. The man, who had offered no name, refilled Vladimir's and his own shot glasses with vodka. It was nothing special. Green Mark shelf vodka—as in the cheapest on the shelf. Long pieces of salty Chechil cheese were piled on a plate in the cheap *pivnaya*. The bar might have been a *kabak* that predated the Russian revolution and not been fixed up since.

The fact that it was inside the closed city of Polyarny should have made it impossible for the American to be here above the Arctic Circle, but he was. Vladimir had dug out his niche here as an engineer designing Russia's nuclear submarines, a cold and lonely banishment far from the shores of the Black Sea.

He raised his glass.

The American raised his own.

After a moment Vladimir offered a toast. "To women."

"And why we love them," the American answered.

They slammed back the shot in unison and each tore off a chunk of cheese. As this wasn't about serious drinking and he didn't know if the man was a friend, he took his time plucking and eating strands of the string cheese.

"I'm hoping you know the missing pieces of my friend's story."

"How much does she know?"

"An arrest, a phone call, and a firebomb."

"So Olga survived." He'd always hoped so even though he remembered her only a little. Sometimes he would accompany his father to his dacha by the Black Sea. He'd been four or five when he'd spent a whole summer vacation there. He remembered the blonde lady. At six he'd lost everything: blonde lady, father, and—soon enough—his mother.

"Not by that name."

"Of course not," this time he refilled their glasses, but didn't reach for his yet. "What I remember most about her was her laugh. She had the most amazing laugh and used it often. I wasn't used to seeing my father happy, but he was with her. I like to think I was with her as well."

The American sat in silence and waited.

"You'd have made a good Russian."

The man's shrug was eloquent. With that as a toast, they both knocked back their glasses.

"I know the phone call. I had my bodyguard place it. Even at six I knew she was in trouble. I begged him to save the 'laughing lady.' I guess his phone call worked."

"She took your father's personal boat and crossed the Black Sea through a winter storm."

Vladimir chewed on that one as he relished the salt from the cheese. There wasn't much flavor to Green Mark vodka, but the salt enhanced what little there was. "I'd forgotten about that boat. It was a very small, open craft, meant for fishing or going along beaches with a picnic. It takes a brave woman to cross the sea in that."

"It does. She laughs less now."

"A *crafty* woman."

The American didn't react at first, then nodded slowly. It confirmed something he'd only guessed at. Olga had been too...alive to be a Russian. So, she too was an American. His father's lover had been an American spy.

Was that what this man across from him was?

He didn't think so. If the American CIA was anything like the KGB or the FSB that had replaced it, then this man should feel less...trustable. Another trait this man shared with his memory of Olga.

Vladimir topped up their glasses. They lifted them in unison, but rather than toasting and drinking, he leaned in, placing his elbows on the scarred old table.

"My mother was sleeping with Gregor, my father's second-in-command. I'm fairly sure that she arranged his wife's death. Together they made up some story about father being the master of a spy ring for the United States.

Funny that it was at least partly true. The purge removed many men, placing Gregor and his cronies in power. He never did marry Mother. She died a couple of years after he tossed her out. She fell asleep drunk outside an illegal bar on the winter night of my eighth birthday."

"And the firebombing of the dacha?"

"Oh, she didn't know about Olga, but the bastard who'd been his friend except for screwing his wife and killing him to get his job, did. My guess would be that Gregor wanted a clean slate." Vladimir didn't wait for a toast, but slugged back the vodka and hissed against the sharp bite.

The American slumped back in his chair.

"Not the story you wanted to hear?"

"It's not that. 'Olga' has spent a lifetime believing it was all her fault."

Vladimir shook his head and the room only blurred a little. "Is that why you are here, or is it about you?" At the man's honest surprise, Vladimir decided he could like this man. "What are *you* regretting, my friend?"

"I'm not sure, but I'm starting to get some ideas. You?"

Vladimir waved his empty glass to encompass the crappy bar in the crappy town above the Arctic Circle, building submarines for a government that was no better than the one that had killed his father and a war that he hoped to God would never happen.

The American nodded and finally drank back his own glass.

Vladimir had doubted this man at first—as expected—but now he saw no more reason to.

"Father gave me something the day before they

executed him by firing squad. Made me promise to give it to Olga if I ever saw her again. Don't know why I grabbed it when you contacted me, but I guess it was the right thing to do." He reached into his coat pocket and slid a small parcel across the table.

The American unwrapped it enough to see what was inside and brushed a finger over its worn surface. He rewrapped it and tucked it in his own pocket before refilling their glasses. He was smiling, which didn't appear to be something he did very often.

Vladimir raised an eyebrow in question as they both raised their glasses.

"Know that, for a brief few years, your father was very happy."

That Vladimir would be glad to drink to.

CHAPTER 9

*D*ilya delivered the package to her library on the same day that news arrived of Michael Gibson finally retiring from Delta Force. Miss Watson approved of his choice of replacement: less of a soldier even if he was Delta, but more of a negotiator.

After more than twenty years of service in the field and two more in command, Michael and his wife were moving to Henderson's Ranch in Montana to have their child. She knew that one way or another, the White House Protection Force be hearing from him soon enough.

The girl had the sensitivity to scoot away quietly. Such sensitivity in that one—she was going to be formidable indeed.

Miss Watson forced herself to complete her row of knitting, careful not to drop any stitches.

Inside the package, there was a card and a small parcel, roughly wrapped.

The card was blank white except for a brief message:

It was Sergei's wife and Gregor.
It wasn't you.

His bitch of a wife and his best friend. They had killed her poor, loving Sergei. He'd brought Gregor to the dacha once for a long-weekend October Revolution Day celebration. It was one of the few times she'd met any of Sergei's people.

And six weeks later Gregor had framed and killed Sergei and tried to firebomb her out of existence. He must have done it so that she could be framed as an American spy without ever being questioned about it thus casting doubt on Gregor's accusations against his friend. Her escape—had it been known about—had been as effective as her death in damning poor Sergei.

His wife and best friend. That was the detail she'd never known. She'd always assumed that it was something she herself had done wrong. It changed everything.

With shaking hands, that wouldn't stop though she ordered them to, she opened the old wrapping paper.

The book was only a little more worn than the last time she'd read it fifty years ago.

It opened easily to where he had pressed a yellow marigold blossom that had been growing close by where they'd first made love. The first time he'd called her his Bright Flower—a nickname that had lasted for three glorious years.

She hadn't cried since hearing of Sergei's death, but now the splashes marked the page.

He *had* loved her like Neruda loved *certain dark things.*

Somehow he'd known what she was— and hadn't cared.

In that tiny space *between shadow and soul.*

And fifty years later he showed her just how grand a thing that was.

OFF THE LEASH

IF YOU ENJOYED THIS, YOU'LL LOVE THE
WHITE HOUSE PROTECTION FORCE
SERIES

OFF THE LEASH (EXCERPT)

WHITE HOUSE PROTECTION FORCE #1

"You're joking."

"Nope. That's his name. And he's yours now."

Sergeant Linda Hamlin wondered quite what it would take to wipe that smile off Lieutenant Jurgen's face. A 120mm round from an M1A1 Abrams Main Battle Tank came to mind.

The kennel master of the US Secret Service's Canine Team was clearly a misogynistic jerk from the top of his polished head to the bottoms of his equally polished boots. She wondered if the shoelaces were polished as well.

Then she looked over at the poor dog sitting hopefully on the concrete kennel floor. His stall had a dog bed three times his size and a water bowl deep enough for him to bathe in. No toys, because toys always came from the handler as a reward. He offered her a sad sigh and a liquid doggy gaze. The kennel even smelled wrong, more of sanitizer than dog. The walls seemed to echo with each bark down the long line of kennels housing the candidate hopefuls for the next addition to the Secret Service's team.

Thor—really?—was a brindle-colored mutt, part who-knew and part no-one-cared. He looked like a cross between an oversized, long-haired schnauzer and a dust mop that someone had spilled dark gray paint on. After mixing in streaks of tawny brown, they'd left one white paw just to make him all the more laughable.

And of course Lieutenant Jerk Jurgen would assign Thor to the first woman on the USSS K-9 team.

Unable to resist, she leaned over far enough to scruff the dog's ears. He was the physical opposite of the sleek and powerful Malinois MWDs—military war dogs—that she'd been handling for the 75th Rangers for the last five years. They twitched with eagerness and nerves. A good MWD was seventy pounds of pure drive—every damn second of the day. If the mild-mannered Thor weighed thirty pounds, she'd be surprised. And he looked like a little girl's best friend who should have a pink bow on his collar.

Jurgen was clearly ex-Marine and would have no respect for the Army. Of course, having been in the Army's Special Operations Forces, she knew better than to respect a Marine.

"We won't let any old swabbie bother us, will we?"

Jurgen snarled—definitely Marine Corps. Swabbie was slang for a Navy sailor and a Marine always took offense at being lumped in with them no matter how much they belonged. Of course the swabbies took offense at having the Marines lumped with *them*. Too bad there weren't any

Navy around so that she could get two for the price of one. Jurgen wouldn't be her boss, so appeasing him wasn't high on her to-do list.

At least she wouldn't need any of the protective bite gear working with Thor. With his stature, he was an explosives detection dog without also being an attack one.

"Where was he trained?" She stood back up to face the beast.

"Private outfit in Montana—some place called Henderson's Ranch. Didn't make their MWD program," his scoff said exactly what he thought the likelihood of any dog outfit in Montana being worthwhile. "They wanted us to try the little runt out."

She'd never heard of a training program in Montana. MWDs all came out of Lackland Air Force Base training. The Secret Service mostly trained their own and they all came from Vohne Liche Kennels in Indiana. Unless… Special Operations Forces dogs were trained by private contractors. She'd worked beside a Delta Force dog for a single month—he'd been incredible.

"Is he trained in English or German?" Most American MWDs were trained in German so that there was no confusion in case a command word happened to be part of a spoken sentence. It also made it harder for any random person on the battlefield to shout something that would confuse the dog.

"German according to his paperwork, but he won't listen to me much in either language."

Might as well give the diminutive Thor a few basic tests. A snap of her fingers and a slap on her thigh had the dog dropping into a smart "heel" position. No need to call out *Fuss—by my foot.*

"*Pass auf!*" *Guard!* She made a pistol with her thumb and forefinger and aimed it at Jurgen as she grabbed her forearm with her other hand—the military hand sign for enemy.

The little dog snarled at Jurgen sharply enough to have him backing out of the kennel. "Goddamn it!"

"*Ruhig.*" *Quiet.* Thor maintained his fierce posture but dropped the snarl.

"*Gute Hund.*" *Good dog,* Linda countered the command.

Thor looked up at her and wagged his tail happily. She tossed him a doggie treat, which he caught midair and crunched happily.

She didn't bother looking up at Jurgen as she knelt once more to check over the little dog. His scruffy fur was so soft that it tickled. Good strength in the jaw, enough to show he'd had bite training despite his size—perfect if she ever needed to take down a three-foot-tall terrorist. Legs said he was a jumper.

"Take your time, Hamlin. I've got nothing else to do with the rest of my goddamn day except babysit you and this mutt."

"Is the course set?"

"Sure. Take him out," Jurgen's snarl sounded almost as nasty as Thor's before he stalked off.

She stood and slapped a hand on her opposite shoulder.

Thor sprang aloft as if he was attached to springs and she caught him easily. He'd cleared well over double his own height. Definitely trained…and far easier to catch than seventy pounds of hyperactive Malinois.

She plopped him back down on the ground. On lead or off? She'd give him the benefit of the doubt and try off first to see what happened.

Linda zipped up her brand-new USSS jacket against the cold and led the way out of the kennel into the hard sunlight of the January morning. Snow had brushed the higher hills around the USSS James J. Rowley Training Center—which this close to Washington, DC, wasn't saying much—but was melting quickly. Scents wouldn't carry as well on the cool air, making it more of a challenge for Thor to locate the explosives. She didn't know where they were either. The course was a test for handler as well as dog.

Jurgen would be up in the observer turret looking for any excuse to mark down his newest team. Perhaps teasing him about being just a Marine hadn't been her best tactical choice. She sighed. At least she was consistent —she'd always been good at finding ways to piss people off before she could stop herself and consider the wisdom of doing so.

This test was the culmination of a crazy three months, so she'd forgive herself this time—something she also wasn't very good at.

In October she'd been out of the Army and unsure what to do next. Tucked in the packet with her DD 214 honorable discharge form had been a flyer on career opportunities with the US Secret Service dog team: *Be all your dog can be!* No one else being released from Fort

Benning that day had received any kind of a job flyer at all that she'd seen, so she kept quiet about it.

She had to pass through DC on her way back to Vermont—her parent's place. Burlington would work for, honestly, not very long at all, but she lacked anywhere else to go after a decade of service. So, she'd stopped off in DC to see what was up with that job flyer. Five interviews and three months to complete a standard six-month training course later—which was mostly a cakewalk after fighting with the US Rangers—she was on-board and this chill January day was her first chance with a dog. First chance to prove that she still had it. First chance to prove that she hadn't made a mistake in deciding that she'd seen enough bloodshed and war zones for one lifetime and leaving the Army.

The Start Here sign made it obvious where to begin, but she didn't dare hesitate to take in her surroundings past a quick glimpse. Jurgen's score would count a great deal toward where she and Thor were assigned in the future. Mostly likely on some field prep team, clearing the way for presidential visits.

As usual, hindsight informed her that harassing the lieutenant hadn't been an optimal strategy. A hindsight that had served her equally poorly with regular Army commanders before she'd finally hooked up with the Rangers—kowtowing to officers had never been one of her strengths.

Thankfully, the Special Operations Forces hadn't given a damn about anything except performance and *that* she could always deliver, since the day she'd been named the team captain for both soccer and volleyball. She was never popular, but both teams had made all-state her last two years in school.

The canine training course at James J. Rowley was a two-acre lot. A hard-packed path of tramped-down dirt led through the brown grass. It followed a predictable pattern from the gate to a junker car, over to tool shed, then a truck, and so on into a compressed version of an intersection in a small town. Beyond it ran an urban street of gray clapboard two- and three-story buildings and an eight-story office tower, all without windows. Clearly a playground for Secret Service training teams.

Her target was the town, so she blocked the city street out of her mind. Focus on the problem: two roads, twenty storefronts, six houses, vehicles, pedestrians.

It might look normal...normalish with its missing windows and no movement. It would be anything but. Stocked with fake IEDs, a bombmaker's stash, suicide cars, weapons caches, and dozens of other traps, all waiting for her and Thor to find. He had to be sensitive to hundreds of scents and it was her job to guide him so that he didn't miss the opportunity to find and evaluate each one.

There would be easy scents, from fertilizer and diesel fuel used so destructively in the 1995 Oklahoma City bombing, to almost as obvious TNT to the very difficult to detect C-4 plastic explosive.

Mannequins on the street carried grocery bags and briefcases. Some held fresh meat, a powerful smell demanding any dog's attention, but would count as a false lead if they went for it. On the job, an explosives detection dog wasn't supposed to care about anything except explosives. Other mannequins were wrapped in suicide vests loaded with Semtex or wearing knapsacks filled with package bombs made from Russian PVV-5A.

She spotted Jurgen stepping into a glassed-in observer turret atop the corner drugstore. Someone else was already there and watching.

She looked down once more at the ridiculous little dog and could only hope for the best.

"Thor?"

He looked up at her.

She pointed to the left, away from the beaten path.

"*Such!*" *Find.*

Thor sniffed left, then right. Then he headed forward quickly in the direction she pointed.

CLIVE ANDREWS SAT in the second-story window at the corner of Main and First, the only two streets in town. Downstairs was a drugstore all rigged to explode, except there were no triggers and there was barely enough explosive to blow up a candy box.

Not that he'd know, but that's what Lieutenant Jurgen had promised him.

It didn't really matter if it was rigged to blow for real, because when Miss Watson—never Ms. or Mrs.—asked for a "favor," you did it. At least he did. Actually, he had yet to meet anyone else who knew her. Not that he'd asked around. She wasn't the sort of person one talked about with strangers, or even close friends. He'd bet even if they did, it would be in whispers. That's just what she was like.

So he'd traveled across town from the White House and into Maryland on a cold winter's morning, barely past a sunrise that did nothing to warm the day. Now he sat in an unheated glass icebox and watched a new officer run a test course he didn't begin to understand.

Keep reading at fine retailers everywhere:
Off the Leash

ABOUT THE AUTHOR

M.L. Buchman started the first of over 60 novels, 75 short stories, and an ever-growing pile of audiobooks while flying from South Korea to ride across the Australian Outback. All part of a solo around-the-world bicycle trip (a mid-life crisis on wheels) that ultimately launched his writing career.

Booklist has selected his military and firefighter series(es) as 3-time "Top 10 Romance of the Year." NPR and Barnes & Noble have named other titles "Top 5 Romance of the Year."

He has flown and jumped out of airplanes, can single-hand a fifty-foot sailboat, and has designed and built two houses. In between writing, he also quilts. M.L. is constantly amazed at what can be done with a degree in geophysics. He also writes: contemporary romance, thrillers, and SF. More info at: www.mlbuchman.com.

Other works by M. L. Buchman:

<u>White House Protection Force</u>
Off the Leash
On Your Mark
In the Weeds

<u>The Night Stalkers</u>
MAIN FLIGHT
The Night Is Mine
I Own the Dawn
Wait Until Dark
Take Over at Midnight
Light Up the Night
Bring On the Dusk
By Break of Day
WHITE HOUSE HOLIDAY
Daniel's Christmas
Frank's Independence Day
Peter's Christmas
Zachary's Christmas
Roy's Independence Day
Damien's Christmas
AND THE NAVY
Christmas at Steel Beach
Christmas at Peleliu Cove
5E
Target of the Heart
Target Lock on Love
Target of Mine
Target of One's Own

<u>Firehawks</u>
MAIN FLIGHT
Pure Heat
Full Blaze
Hot Point
Flash of Fire
Wild Fire
SMOKEJUMPERS
Wildfire at Dawn
Wildfire at Larch Creek
Wildfire on the Skagit

<u>Delta Force</u>
Target Engaged
Heart Strike
Wild Justice
Midnight Trust

<u>Where Dreams</u>
Where Dreams are Born
Where Dreams Reside
Where Dreams Are of Christmas
Where Dreams Unfold
Where Dreams Are Written

<u>Eagle Cove</u>
Return to Eagle Cove
Recipe for Eagle Cove
Longing for Eagle Cove
Keepsake for Eagle Cove

<u>Henderson's Ranch</u>
Nathan's Big Sky
Big Sky, Loyal Heart
Big Sky Dog Whisperer

<u>Love Abroad</u>
Heart of the Cotswolds: England
Path of Love: Cinque Terre, Italy

<u>Dead Chef Thrillers</u>
Swap Out!
One Chef!
Two Chef!

<u>Deities Anonymous</u>
Cookbook from Hell: Reheated
Saviors 101

<u>SF/F Titles</u>
The Nara Reaction
Monk's Maze
the Me and Elsie Chronicles

<u>Strategies for Success (NF)</u>
Managing Your Inner Artist/Writer
Estate Planning for Authors

Short Story Series by M. L. Buchman:

The Night Stalkers
The Night Stalkers
The Night Stalkers 5E
The Night Stalkers CSAR
The Night Stalkers Wedding Stories

Firehawks
The Firehawks Lookouts
The Firehawks Hotshots
The Firebirds

Delta Force
Delta Force Short Stories

US Coast Guard
US Coast Guard

White House Protection Force
White House Protection Force Short Stories

Where Dreams
Where Dreams Short Stories

Eagle Cove
Eagle Cove Short Story

Henderson's Ranch
Henderson's Ranch Short Stories

Dead Chef Thrillers
Dead Chef Short Stories

Deities Anonymous
Deities Anonymouse Short Stories

SF/F Titles
The Future Night Stalkers
Single Titles

SIGN UP FOR M. L. BUCHMAN'S NEWSLETTER TODAY

and receive:
Release News
Free Short Stories
a Free Book

Get your free book today. Do it now.
free-book.mlbuchman.com